SUSAN STEGGALL

trained as a graphic designer at Bath College
of Higher Education before becoming a school teacher.
It was her boys, and their fascination with vehicles of all kinds,
that gave her the inspiration for *On The Road*.
This is her first book for Frances Lincoln.

For Oscar, Ralph and Paul with love,
and with special thanks to the man in the Land Rover.

On the Road copyright © Frances Lincoln Limited 2005
Text and illustrations copyright © Susan Steggall 2005

First published in Great Britain in 2005
by Frances Lincoln Children's Books, 4 Torriano Mews,
Torriano Avenue, London NW5 2RZ

www.franceslincoln.com

First paperback edition published in 2006

British Library Cataloguing in Publication Data
available on request

ISBN 1-84507-491-2
Printed in China

1 3 5 7 9 8 6 4 2

ON THE
ROAD

Susan Steggall

FRANCES LINCOLN CHILDREN'S BOOKS

Off we go

along the road

past the garage

up the hill

around the corner

through the roadworks

STOP!

Down the hill

into the tunnel

across the junction

under the bridge

over the fields

to the sea!

MORE TITLES FROM FRANCES LINCOLN CHILDREN'S BOOKS

The Day the Baby Blew Away

Simon Puttock

Illustrated by Cathy Gale

When the wind spies Mama and Papa's beautiful baby,
it whisks her away across the town, causing havoc everywhere they go.
The baby will not stop crying, even when the wind steals
old Mrs McGinty's shawl to keep her warm. Luckily Grandpa
and his lasso are there to save the day.

ISBN 1-84507-119-0

Help!

Chris Inns

There is no time to rest when you are
on call at the toy hospital. Doctor Hopper and Nurse Rex Barker
have to be ready for every emergency. You never know
when they might have to jump into their ambulance, or when they will hear
a toy in trouble on the radio, shouting, "HELP!"

ISBN 1-84507-123-9

Brave Mouse

Michaela Morgan

Illustrated by Michelle Cartledge

Lots of things frighten Little Mouse: dark shadows, bright lights,
loud noises. Sometimes he doesn't want to do things
the other little mice do, and they tease him and call him a scaredy-mouse.
This is the charming tale of how Little Mouse learns
to stand up for himself, and how being able to say NO
to your friends can make you very brave indeed!

ISBN 1-84507-129-8

Frances Lincoln titles are available from all good bookshops.
You can also buy books and find out more about your favourite titles, authors
and illustrators on our website: www.franceslincoln.com